TRAPPED!

A Search-and-Rescue Dog Story

by Meish Goldish

illustrated by David Malan

BEARPORT
PUBLISHING

New York, New York

Credits
Cover photo, © Grisha Bruev/Shutterstock.

Publisher: Kenn Goin
Editor: Jessica Rudolph
Creative Director: Spencer Brinker

Library of Congress Cataloging-in-Publication Data

Names: Goldish, Meish, author.
Title: Trapped! A Search-and-Rescue Dog Story/ by Meish Goldish.
Description: New York, New York : Bearport Publishing, [2017] I Series: Hound
    Town Chronicles I Summary: Search-and-rescue dogs are used to find three
    students and a teacher when they become trapped in the basement of an
    elementary school following an explosion.
Identifiers: LCCN 2016043995 (print) I LCCN 2016053783 (ebook) I ISBN
    9781684020188 (library) I ISBN 9781684020690 (ebook)
Subjects: I CYAC: Search dogs—Fiction. I Rescue dogs—Fiction. I
    Dogs—Fiction. I Rescues—Fiction.
Classification: LCC PZ7.1.M479 Tr 2017 (print) I LCC PZ7.1.M479 (ebook) I DDC
    [E]—dc23
LC record available at https://lccn.loc.gov/2016043995

For more information, write to Bearport Publishing Company, Inc., 45 West
21st Street, Suite 3B, New York, New York 10010. Printed in the United States
of America.

10 9 8 7 6 5 4 3 2 1

CONTENTS

WELCOME TO **HOUND TOWN**

A Doggone Nice Place to Live!

Population:
25,000 people
20,000 dogs

CHAPTER 1

BOOM!

"Hey, Sparky, fetch the ball," said ten-year-old Jimmy. He softly kicked a soccer ball across the gym floor toward a small, white poodle.

Sparky scurried away and hid behind his owner, Mr. Brady. The dog let out an *Arf* and eyed the rolling ball **warily** as it slowly came to a stop. Jimmy and all the students around him laughed.

Mr. Brady chuckled, too. "All right, everyone, let's start the first meeting of the Dog **Obedience** Club. For the first few meetings, we'll work with my dog, Sparky, to learn the basic **commands**. Later on, you can bring in your own dogs."

It was a cold winter afternoon at Hound Town Elementary School. Classes were over for the day. Everyone was out of the building except for the members of the club.

The students sat on the bleachers facing Mr. Brady, the fourth-grade science teacher. Jimmy raised his hand. "Mr. Brady," he said, "my dog, Apollo, doesn't always listen when I want him to come to me."

"I sometimes have that problem with Sparky," Mr. Brady replied. "He's young and still learning, and he gets **distracted**."

"So what do you do?" asked ten-year-old club member Melissa.

Mr. Brady bent down and petted Sparky as he spoke. "You must be gentle but firm. Let your dog know by the sound of your voice when you're happy or unhappy with its behavior."

Mr. Brady then said, "Sparky, sit." The canine sat, tilted his head, and looked up at his owner.

"Now for the trickier part," said Mr. Brady, smiling.

The students watched as Mr. Brady walked backward a few paces and stopped. Then the teacher said, "Sparky, come."

Sparky hesitated. He looked at the students, then at the soccer ball a few feet away.

"Sparky, come!" said Mr. Brady, this time even more firmly.

The poodle began to walk toward his owner. Suddenly, there was a terrible noise. *BOOM!* A powerful explosion tore apart the gym floor. Everyone screamed and covered their heads as pieces of the bleachers flew everywhere!

A section of the wooden floorboards collapsed. The five students, along with Mr. Brady and Sparky, **plummeted** down into the school

basement one floor below. Smoke and dust filled the air. No one knew it at the time, but the school's gas **boiler** had just exploded.

Jimmy lay on his back, covered by wooden boards and other **debris**. He slowly moved his hands around and felt something soft under his body. He was lying on a pile of gym mats. His eyes stung from the dust-filled air. He coughed, trying to clear his dry throat. "Hello? Can anybody hear me?" he asked weakly.

Melissa whispered, "Yes, I can hear you."

Jimmy felt sore all over, but he managed to crawl out from under the blanket of debris and stand up. He tried to find Melissa, yet it was too dark and smoky to see much.

Jimmy squinted his eyes. "Melissa, where are you?" he asked.

"Over here," she said. "I'm right here."

He followed the sound of her voice. After walking a few steps, he bumped into her feet. "Oh!" he cried. "Are you okay?"

Melissa coughed. "I think so," she said. "Can you help me?"

Jimmy bent down and slowly pulled Melissa out from under the pile of boards that covered her. Then he helped her stand up. "What happened?" Melissa asked, dusting herself off.

"I'm not sure," Jimmy said. "I think something exploded."

"Where are the others?" Melissa asked.

"I don't know," Jimmy said. "You're the first one I found."

Melissa began to shake nervously. "We've got to find everyone," she said. "We need to know if they're okay."

Melissa tried to walk, but she bumped into something in the darkness. "Ow! I wish we had a flashlight," she said.

"Yeah," said Jimmy. Then, from the corner of his eye, he saw sunlight creeping into the smoky room from a tiny crack in the building. "Hey look, there's light over there!" he cried. "Come on."

Jimmy and Melissa shuffled toward the light. As they got closer, they could see their surroundings a little better.

"There are some old red gym mats piled up here," Jimmy said. "That's what we landed on. We must be in the school basement."

"I hope the others landed on mats, too," Melissa said. "Or else they could be really hurt. Let's try to find them."

CHAPTER 2

A Way Out?

Jimmy and Melissa climbed over steel beams and chunks of **concrete**, occasionally coughing up dust. Every few seconds, they called out to the others. "Mr. Brady! . . . Holly?" There was no reply.

"Where are they?" Melissa asked uneasily. "Why won't they answer?"

What she and Jimmy didn't know was that two of the students, Marcus and Meiko, were knocked **unconscious** by the blast. The third student, Holly, and Mr. Brady were awake but too **dazed** to respond to the calls.

"Okay, I'm getting really scared. We've got to get help," Jimmy said. "Do you have your cell phone?"

Melissa felt her empty pockets. "No," she replied. "I think it was sitting on the bleachers when the blast happened. My phone is probably buried somewhere here in the basement."

"Mine, too," Jimmy said. "There's no way we'll find them in this mess. Let's just follow the light in that corner. If sunlight is getting in, maybe we can escape through that opening."

Slowly, Jimmy and Melissa continued to make their way toward the light. Then they began to move pieces of debris away from the tiny opening in the building. After a few minutes, they heard a familiar sound.

Woof! Woof!

"Wait, is that Sparky? It doesn't sound like him," Melissa said.

"It's coming from up there," Jimmy said, pointing up to the crack in the building above their heads.

Melissa grabbed Jimmy's arm. "Look!" she gasped. "There's a dog up there!"

Jimmy saw a golden retriever looking down through the small hole. The dog sniffed and then barked again.

Woof!

A person's voice called from above, "Is anybody down there? Are you injured?"

"Help! There are two of us. Melissa and Jimmy. We're okay!" Melissa shouted.

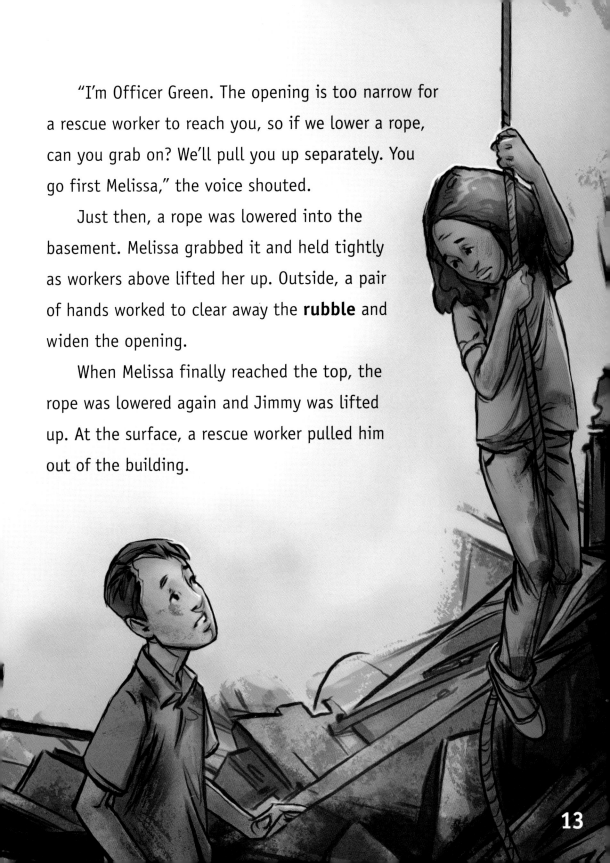

"I'm Officer Green. The opening is too narrow for a rescue worker to reach you, so if we lower a rope, can you grab on? We'll pull you up separately. You go first Melissa," the voice shouted.

Just then, a rope was lowered into the basement. Melissa grabbed it and held tightly as workers above lifted her up. Outside, a pair of hands worked to clear away the **rubble** and widen the opening.

When Melissa finally reached the top, the rope was lowered again and Jimmy was lifted up. At the surface, a rescue worker pulled him out of the building.

"We're outside!" Jimmy cried. He and Melissa breathed in the cold air and looked around. The two students couldn't believe what they saw. Parts of the school's walls and ceiling had collapsed. Gray smoke filled the sky. Emergency vehicles surrounded the scene—police cars, fire trucks, and ambulances.

Just then, the two students saw their parents, who had rushed to the scene after hearing news of the explosion. "Are you all right?" Jimmy's mother asked. Jimmy and Melissa assured everyone that they were fine. The parents hugged their children and put coats on them to warm them up.

Two ambulance workers approached Jimmy and Melissa to make sure they had no serious injuries.

The children were glad to be safe, but were worried. Would the others who were still trapped in the basement be rescued?

CHAPTER 3

The Search Begins

A police officer approached Jimmy and Melissa. "I'm Officer Sarah Green," she said. "I helped pull you out of the building. Are there others still down there?"

"Yes," Melissa said. "There are three more students—Marcus, Meiko, and Holly—plus Mr. Brady and his dog."

"We don't know where they are," Jimmy added. "They never called back when we shouted out to them." As he thought about his friends lying underneath the rubble, Jimmy held back tears.

Officer Green asked, "Can you show me where you think *you* landed underground?" Jimmy looked at the building opening where they had escaped. Then he walked about fifty feet with the officer.

"I think we landed down there," Jimmy said, pointing to a part of the damaged building.

"Thank you," said Officer Green. Then she waved to two nearby police officers with dogs. "Over here!" she called.

The two officers and their dogs approached. Officer Green introduced them. Officer John Shire stood with his German shepherd, Spotter. Officer Tom Casey was with Rudy, a golden retriever.

Officer Green said, "These police officers are **handlers** who work

with our **search-and-rescue dogs**. Rudy is the dog who found the two of you. The dogs will try to find the scents of the other **victims**, too."

"Hi, Spotter. Hi, Rudy," said Melissa.

Jimmy knelt down in front of the dogs. Spotter had a strong, confident expression. Rudy's tongue was hanging out, and he looked very sweet. "Thanks for finding us. I hope you can find our friends, too." Looking at the dogs, Jimmy began to feel hopeful that everyone would be found.

Then, Officers Casey and Shire each gave the command "Search!" as they pointed to the building. Immediately, Rudy and Spotter began to sniff the rubble. Spotter darted around quickly. Rudy worked a little slower, being more careful around the sharp-edged debris.

Jimmy and Melissa watched the dogs work. "Why do you use dogs?" Melissa asked Officer Green. "Can't officers find missing people?"

"Not always," Officer Green explained. "A SAR dog—that's what we call a search-and-rescue dog—can search a large area much faster than a human can. And a dog is amazing at picking up a scent."

"But can SAR dogs smell people way under all that rubble?" Jimmy asked.

"Yes," Officer Green replied. "They can smell someone who's as far as thirty feet under the surface."

"What if the dogs smell someone?" Jimmy asked. "Will they go down into the basement to look for them?"

"That's our plan," Officer Green answered, pointing to a nearby truck. "This vehicle is clearing away debris to make an opening for the dogs to enter. Then, when the opening is even bigger, human rescuers will follow them."

"Is it dangerous for the dogs?" Melissa asked.

"Don't worry," Officer Green replied. "Rudy and Spotter are well trained. They can walk on narrow beams without losing their balance. They can crawl through small spaces, too. These dogs aren't afraid to go anywhere their noses lead them."

Just then, the German shepherd began to bark loudly. "Spotter's found someone!" Officer Shire cried.

19

CHAPTER 4

Cold and Dark

A group of rescue workers gathered at the spot where Spotter had been barking. A steam shovel began to remove concrete blocks and steel beams piled on the ground.

The late-afternoon sun was starting to set, and the temperature was dropping. Jimmy whispered to Melissa nervously, "I hope the rescue workers find them soon. They might freeze down there."

"Don't worry, the workers will find them," Melissa said.

Minutes later, Rudy began to bark in another spot nearby. More workers rushed to that area. The piles of debris were not as high there. So, the workers used shovels and their hands to clear away the rubble as quickly as possible.

Jimmy and Melissa watched the activity with their parents and Officer Green. "It looks like both dogs have picked up scents," the officer said. "That's a very good sign."

Soon, both areas were clear enough for the dogs to crawl down into the basement. The handlers stayed outside and yelled commands to the canines. "Go!" they called. "Search!"

Both Rudy and Spotter squeezed through the small openings, each one walking along steel beams.

Outside, police officers and other rescue workers waited anxiously. "How will you know if the dogs find anyone down there?" Melissa asked Officer Green.

"They'll tell us by barking," she replied. "Or they may return with an item that belongs to one of the victims."

After a few minutes, Spotter started to climb out of the basement, and Officer Shire helped lift him to the surface. Spotter held a red baseball cap in his mouth. "That's Marcus's cap!" Jimmy cried.

Officer Shire took the cap and hugged the German shepherd. "Good girl!"

Rudy still had not returned. "Where do you think Rudy is?" Melissa asked.

"I hope he's not hurt," Jimmy said.

As the sun set, the air grew even colder. Rescuers worked quickly to make the building openings large enough for people to fit through.

At last, enough debris was cleared away. Officers Shire and Casey went down into the basement with Spotter. The officers searched the dark area with flashlights. Soon they heard the sounds of Rudy's barks, along with weak voices crying, "Help! Help!" The officers' flashlights revealed four people and a small white dog scattered on gym mats. Rudy was standing nearby, wagging his tail.

"Rudy found you!" Officer Casey cried. "Good boy, Rudy!" By now, all the victims were awake, but they were bruised, sore, and shivering. In the explosion, Meiko had suffered a broken arm, and Marcus had a large cut on his leg.

Firefighters dropped blankets down into the basement, and the officers placed the blankets on everyone to warm them up. Then the officers bandaged Meiko's arm and Marcus's leg. "Now, let's get everyone out of here!" Officer Shire ordered.

"Wait, what about Jimmy and Melissa?" asked Mr. Brady.

"The dogs already found them, just like they found you," said Officer Casey, smiling. "They're safe and sound."

Soon, a rescue **hoist** was lowered into the basement. It looked like a large cloth bag held by a hook. The officers gently placed Marcus into the cloth seat.

A fire truck operator pulled the hook up, slowly lifting Marcus to the surface. Firefighters carefully removed Marcus from the hoist. Then the truck operator lowered it back into the basement to retrieve the other victims one by one.

After a few minutes, all three students were safely outside. That left Mr. Brady and Sparky in the basement, along with the two police officers and their SAR dogs.

Officer Shire bent down to pick up Sparky. The dog's eyes widened, and he backed away. Then the frightened dog quickly darted toward a corner of the basement. The police officers used their flashlights to search for the dog.

Mr. Brady called loudly. "Sparky, come here!" he commanded. "Come right now!" But Sparky didn't move. Instead, the scared little dog remained in the corner behind a large pile of debris.

"Okay, Mr. Brady," Officer Casey said, "you ride up in the hoist. We'll bring your dog up."

Mr. Brady hesitated. "Please," he said, "promise you'll get my dog out safely."

The officers smiled. "Don't worry, sir, we'll get him," Officer Casey said. Then he placed Mr. Brady in the hoist.

CHAPTER 5

The Final Rescue

Officers Shire and Casey moved closer to the corner where Sparky was hiding. They continued to call the dog's name. "Come, Sparky!" they commanded. It didn't work. Sparky remained hidden.

By now, the basement was completely dark except for the lights from the officers' flashlights.

Just then, Rudy and Spotter walked to the debris in the corner where Sparky was hiding. They got down on their bellies and crawled under the broken boards. Only their back legs and tails were visible. The officers heard the two canines whimper softly. Suddenly, Spotter began to howl—*Aaaoooooohh*. She sounded like a wolf!

A tiny figure slowly **emerged** from the debris with Rudy and Spotter. It was Sparky! He confidently trotted alongside the bigger dogs. All three were covered in dust.

Officer Shire picked up Sparky and held the poodle tightly with one arm. Then he bent down and petted Spotter with his other arm. "Good girl!" he cried. "You calmed him down."

Officer Casey hugged Rudy. "Good boy!" he said.

Officer Shire walked back to the hoist with Sparky. Together, they rode up to ground level.

Outside, Mr. Brady hugged his poodle and shouted, "Sparky, you're all right!" Then he thanked Officer Shire.

After Officer Casey and the SAR dogs were lifted to the surface, Officer Shire counted everyone to make sure all were safely out of the building. "Everyone's here!" he declared.

Jimmy walked over to Officer Shire. "Why did it take so long to get Sparky out of the building?" he asked.

Officer Shire smiled. "We had to wait for the SAR dogs to work their magic. They managed to do what we humans couldn't do. They got the scared poodle to leave his hiding place."

By now, all the students' parents were hugging their children tightly, all asking the same question: "Are you okay?"

Ambulance workers checked each disaster victim. Jimmy, Melissa, Holly, and Mr. Brady had only scratches and bruises. Marcus and Meiko had each suffered a mild **concussion** in the explosion but had no serious head wounds. Marcus's cut leg was washed and wrapped in fresh bandages. Only Meiko had to go to the hospital, where a cast was put on her broken arm.

The next day, the newspaper headline in the *Hound Town Chronicles* read: "Dogs Help Rescue 6 People—Plus One of Their Own—in School Gas Explosion."

The news article described the event in great detail and included interviews with each of the students who had been rescued.

In the article, Melissa said, "We were really lucky that we had brave police officers and their dogs to help us."

DOGS HELP RESCUE 6 PEOPLE
—Plus One of Their Own—in School Gas Explosion

In the same article, Jimmy said, "When I grow up, I want to be a handler for a search-and-rescue dog. SAR dogs are amazing. They save people's lives—and animals' lives, too!"

A photo in the newspaper article showed Jimmy with his arms around Spotter and Rudy, and a big smile on his face.

Trapped!
A Search-and-Rescue Dog Story

1. In what ways were Jimmy and Melissa lucky after the explosion took place?

2. What is happening in this scene?

3. How do Rudy and Spotter prove that they are well trained for their jobs?

4. How is Sparky rescued at the end of the story?

5. Imagine that you are a search-and-rescue dog handler. What do you think would be the best part of your job? What might be the hardest part?

boiler (BOI-lur) a tank in which water is heated or hot water is stored

commands (kuh-MANDZ) orders given to an animal by a person

concrete (kahn-KREET) a mixture of sand, water, cement, and gravel that is used in construction

concussion (kuhn-KUSH-uhn) a temporary brain injury caused by a blow to the head

dazed (DAYZD) stunned and unable to think clearly

debris (duh-BREE) scattered pieces of buildings or other objects that have been broken or destroyed

distracted (diss-TRAKT-id) having one's attention drawn away by something

emerged (ih-MURJD) came out from somewhere hidden

handlers (HAND-lurz) people who help to train or manage dogs

hoist (HOIST) a machine used to lift or raise something

obedience (oh-BEE-dee-uhnss) the act of following good behavior and rules

plummeted (PLUHM-ih-tid) fell quickly

rubble (RUHB-uhl) broken pieces of rock, brick, and other building materials

search-and-rescue dogs (SURCH-AND-RES-kyoo DAWGZ) dogs that look for survivors after a disaster

unconscious (uhn-KAHN-shuhss) not awake; unable to see, feel, or think

victims (VIK-tuhmz) people or animals who are injured or killed

warily (WARE-ih-lee) cautiously

About the Author

Meish Goldish is an award-winning author of more than 300 books for children. His book *City Firefighters* won a Teachers' Choice Award in 2015. He especially enjoys writing fiction, nonfiction, and poetry about animals. Growing up in Tulsa, Oklahoma, Meish liked to play with the many dogs in his neighborhood. Now a resident of Brooklyn, New York, he continues to frolic among the friendly canines there.

About the Illustrator

David Malan has always been an artist. It began with pencils and paper and reprimands from schoolteachers. This led to his career as an illustrator, drawing faces, painting pictures of his kids, and digitally illustrating whatever can be dreamed up. Today, he happily paints in his basement and then enjoys spending time with his wife and four young kids. He sits back down to draw after they go to bed.